Courting The Winter Prince

LIANA BROOKS

OTHER WORKS

HEROES AND VILLAINS

Even Villains Fall In Love
Even Villains Go To The Movies
Even Villains Have Interns
Even Villains Play The Hero (books 1 – 3 omnibus)
The Polar Terror

FLEET OF MALIK

Bodies In Motion
Change of Momentum
For Every Action (forthcoming)

SHORTER WORKS

All I Want For Christmas Is A Werewolf
Fey Lights
Prime Sensations
Darkness and Good

Find other works by the author at
www.lianabrooks.com

Courting The Winter Prince

INKLET #34

LIANA BROOKS

Inkprint
PRESS

www.inkprintpress.com

Print ISBN: 978-1-925825-33-6
eBook ISBN: 9781393767121

www.inkprintpress.com

National Library of Australia Cataloguing-in-Publication Data
Brooks, Liana 1982 –
Courting The Winter Prince
42 p.
ISBN: 978-1-925825-33-6
Inkprint Press, Canberra, Australia
1. Fiction—Fairy Tales, Folk Tales, Legends & Mythology
2. Fiction—Fantasy—Romantic 3. Fiction—Short Stories

First Print Edition: May 2020
Cover photo © Pexels via Pixabay
Cover design © Inkprint Press
Interior art © Amy Laurens

COURTING THE WINTER PRINCE

IT WASN'T A STORYBOOK ROMANCE. NOT in the way people imagined.

There was no fairy godmother. No magical mice. Nothing but a few dusty gowns hanging in the attic and stolen, midnight moments stitching a dream by candlelight.

I wasn't sure if anyone would understand if I tried to explain why I needed to go to the ball. It wasn't for the dress. It certainly wasn't because I thought I should have a crown.

I did it for friendship... and love.

Years ago, just after mother died, I ran deep into the woods, driven half by sorrow and half by despair. In the deep, mountain woods that smelled of rain, and earth, and pine, there was a meadow of flowers where I could cry. I pictured my bones there, bleached by the sun and shrouded by the brown dress that was all that remained of my family's fortune. Everything else had been sold to buy medicine for mother. To buy hope. To buy time.

He found me there, in the dead of night, a wide-eyed boy who'd been thrown by his horse and gotten lost in the woods.

I lived because he wanted to go home, because he said it was important. I knew the woods well and by morning I was hungry and thirsty enough to stop weeping long enough to save a stranger.

He asked me to meet him again.

Curiosity brought me back to the woods a second time. To meet a fey-like boy who told stories of towering castles and knights. I loved his stories.

He made me laugh.

In time, as my world changed, my father re-married, the boy in the woods was the only one who could make me smile. He taught me to dance because my step-mother said she couldn't afford to pay the tutor for three students. He taught me to sing.

And one summery day when the meadow was thick with the scent of honey-suckle and the buzz of bees, he taught me to kiss.

Our friendship had become something more.

We laughed, and we talked, and he was half my soul...

And then I saw the invitation. The prince was giving a ball.

The man I loved wasn't a simple person like me, but the crown prince, heir to thrones and palaces. The stories he'd told me weren't from books at all.

I had to go up to the attic, with the little window that had a view of the palace through the empty branches of winter trees.

I had to sew my dress.

Had to use those dusty gowns that were the finest fabric in the house, re-stitching them into something new, something a girl in a forest would never wear.

I had to see him one last time. To say goodbye. To wish him well. To know he was married to someone who would protect him if he were ever lost in the woods again.

The night air was sultry, scented with jasmine and the brine of the nearby sea.

The palace glowed, golden domes lit by torches, polished marble floors shimmering in the firelight.

The people were beautiful. My step-sisters looked like angels. The men looked all looked like heroes.

I felt so small, in a simple dress of plain spring green. I'd woven flowers into my hair because I had no jewels and my shoes were the simple leather ones I wore at home. But he danced with me all the same.

Only once, very early in the evening, and I whispered my goodbyes as I bowed. Wished him well with a tear in my eye.

I watched as the beautiful princess in the magical blue gown came. I saw the sparkling shoes on her feet. I gasped when she ran at midnight.

And I alone saw the prince look back at me before he ran to chase after the maiden fair.

In the weeks that followed, everyone talked about the Princess-To-Be. They gossiped and whispered and my step-sisters cried with joy when they heard the prince would visit each house looking for his lost True Love.

I went to the woods to be alone. He wasn't there. He was chasing a princess fair.

I went home and sat by the dovecot, the taste of dust thick in my throat. I had never been so naive that I had dreamed of happily ever after. I had asked for nothing, and the world had given me nothing.

There were stolen moments of joy—more, perhaps, than anyone had a right to. Those stolen moments in the woods where my whole universe was his smile as he listened, as we talked, as he didn't say the words that matched the emotions in his eyes.

But that was all I'd ever expected.

The leaves were changing colors when the prince's retinue rode up to our house on the edge of the wood. My father was first to greet him, then he introduced my step-mother and step-sisters. I stood with the servants, eyes on the ground.

The prince's companions made a great show of greeting everyone, although I did not like the look in the duke's eye as he smiled at the scullery maid. One raised eyebrow and the prince called him away, sending him to care for his horse.

I should have guessed what was happening then. Across the hazy courtyard filled with dust and confusion, all it took was one look for him to understand.

Still, I was shocked when the prince knelt before me and slid a slipper of gold and mirrors on my foot. It fit perfectly. As if made for me.

Everyone gasped.

"It's not possible," I whispered.

The corner of his lip lifted in a secret smile. "Parties aren't the only place women can lose shoes. Last summer you went barefoot for a month."

"I only ever found the one sandal," I said slowly. Down by the creek where we sometimes swam.

The prince stood, eyes alight, taking my hand. "I have found my Queen! She is the woman I danced with at the ball who has run away with my heart!"

The retainers looked at me in shock, but it couldn't rival the confusion on my father's face. I hadn't worn a mask to the ball. Everyone in the family had seen me.

"Ah, my liege," my father sputtered. "Are you quite certain?"

"Absolutely certain." There was a challenge in the prince's eye, one I knew joyously well, but that put fear into everyone around us. "Do you object, my love?"

"To loving you?" I asked. "Never. You have my heart."

He always would. He'd saved my life and brought me happiness. Given me more than all the money in the world could buy. He'd given me a life after death.

It was said later that the Winter Prince had found his heart in summer. Though the prophecies said he would grow to be a cruel tyrant, he was tempered by the love of a princess with flowers in her hair. They said my love saved him, changed him, redeemed him.

If only they knew the truth...

THE MAKING OF *COURTING THE WINTER PRINCE*

"Cinderella with a twist." That's all the plot I had. And I've done Cinderella With A Twist before (Inklet #40, *Not Quite Cinderella,* which was written before this one despite the release order).

But this time I wanted something playful, something hopeful, something that combined Cinderella and Persephone.

And here we are. A Summer Queen and a Winter Prince, forever dancing together.

Read more by Liana Brooks!

FLEET OF MALIK: BODIES IN MOTION
CHAPTER ONE

THE PROBLEM WITH VACATIONS, Selena reflected as she adjusted her sweater outside Cargo Blue, was that reality was always waiting at the end. A quick search of the local security cameras found one that showed the peeling sunburn on her right shoulder blade.

Such was the curse of pale-skinned, ship-born Fleet personnel. Anytime she left the foggy belts covering the city of Tarrin, she barbecued like a shrimp, no matter how much sunscreen she applied. Otherwise, she'd flee even further from the Fleet Enclave and make her home on the equatorial beaches of the planet they were trapped on.

She panned the camera and checked her left shoulder. Black ink made a star-scape that disguised three silver scars as shooting stars. The painting covered her shoulder blade and part of her upper arm. As the artist had promised, the skin-paint had kept her from burning as much, though it still had the over-stretched feel of a burn. With a few adjustments, her uniform covered most of the temporary art; it would keep her from having to explain to her colleagues.

Her forearm warmed, a warning that someone was about to contact her through the tech implant tucked between her radius and ulna.

She hesitated too long and the call came through, a persistent ping against her skull as the phantom image of her best friend floated on the edge of her vision.

Selena turned off the visual receiver and answered. "Genevieve," she said with a smile as the image of her vivacious, red-headed friend appeared floating against the backdrop of landing gear that supported the grounded fleet.

A grounder would have thought she was talking to herself, but grounders wouldn't set foot near the neo-city-state of

Enclave. The rocky beach served as a city and tomb for the survivors of the last war.

"Selena!" Gen gushed. "Starcom to Selena. Where are you? I'm covering for now."

"Delayed, but almost there." Selena hoped Gen wouldn't hear the lie. She'd been standing in the shadows of the Enclave pub for nearly a quarter hour.

"The *Lorenza* could get here faster," Gen said, referencing a long-dead ship whose crew were found skeletonized at their stations. Gen blew hair off her face. "Stars above, you're an hour late. The whole fleet is flying faster than you."

Selena turned on her visual long enough to roll her eyes at her friend. "Ha, ha, funny. That joke needs to be forcibly retired." Sooner rather than later. The fleet couldn't fly without fuel, and the Malik system they were stranded in held precious few deposits of the orun crystals needed to power the ships.

"If you don't come," Gen said threateningly, "I will teleport to your apartment and drag you out in your pajamas."

"I'm not at home," Selena admitted. And she wouldn't have let her best friend come to her new house if she was.

Gen was smart enough to realize that the small palace Selena had bought in downtown Tarrin wasn't paid for by her official OIA salary. The paygrades for the Office of Imperial Affairs had last been updated when the Malik system was still in contact with the empire, making them 900 years out of date.

Technically, taking a second job wasn't treason, but there were enough people in the fleet who'd see it as a betrayal that keeping it secret felt right. Especially since Gen's captain was one who would scream the loudest.

Gen clapped. "Selena! Stop stalling yer engines and get in here. This isn't some Fleet Tribunal, just our friends. You, me, Carver. I left a message for Marshall. You know. People we like."

The light of understanding dawned. "Carver? This is so you can snuggle up to Perrin Carver without your parents watching?"

"Yes," Gen admitted, not looking the least bit contrite.

"You're only dragging me along so I can cover for you while you make out in a corner, aren't you?" She masked the relief with mock anger. At least Gen wasn't trying to set Selena up with one of her cousins. Or, ancestors forbid, Gen's handsy older brother.

Again.

Gen opened her eyes wide with an innocent smile. "Maybe."

"Gen!" Selena rolled her eyes. "Doesn't he have his own place?"

"Just the bachelor's dorm. The Carvers didn't have any ships except the shuttle his parents crashed in. Making out next door to Mom and Dad? No. And the BOQ? It's so tacky. You can hear everything through those walls."

Selena hid a smile. "I'll be there soon enough."

If Gen ever caught wind of how panicky the thought of a relationship made her, Gen would make it her life's goal to see Selena paired off. And there wasn't a man alive who she could imagine getting close to now.

Her implant helpfully pulled up an image of a tall, broad-shouldered, lean-muscled fighter with skin black as the night between stars and emerald-green eyes.

She pushed the memory away.

Lieutenant Commander Titan Sciarra was striking, intelligent, and had a body she'd cross battle lines for, but he was also out of reach. There was no point in chasing a man who wouldn't give her the time of day.

Another crew shuffled past her into the bar, black patches with silver fists on their shoulders.

It was getting harder to pretend she belonged in Enclave, with the fleet. Once upon a time, she'd known every crew's patch without thinking. She could name captains, their ships and their seconds by rote.

Now she would need to tap into the fleet's information nexus if she wanted to know who they were.

She stopped at the edge of the door to tug her lightest shields into place. A few minor adjustments would keep bugs away, keep beer off her clothes, and prevent anyone from hacking into her implant. They could still send messages, because disallowing that would have raised eyebrows. And they could still hit her. But she could always hit back.

Selena rolled her shoulders and strutted into Cargo Blue. It was a battlefield, but she was the last captain of the Caryll family, and she wasn't going down without a fight.

Whatever crew owned Cargo Blue probably hadn't had much of a decorating budget, but at least they'd stuck with a theme: oversized cargo boxes were piled up to make walls, seating, and tables. Olive-green safety webbing draped from the ceiling between blue lights. Fog used for fire drills on the ships pumped across the floor to hide the concrete beneath.

There was no bouncer at the door, but people were still hanging around the entrance.

As a rule, the fleet was cautious, and the young faces she saw belonged to fleet members who had never ventured outside their own crew more than a few times, even though the fleet had been grounded for nearly three years.

Tables to the left, bar ahead, dance floor to the right... and that meant the back half of the cargo hanger had been partitioned and karaoke would be in the back right corner. After a few minutes of weaving through the human crush, she found Gen, already sitting in Perrin Carver's lap and giggling.

"Selena!" Gen jumped up and hugged her. "I was beginning to worry!"

"How many people are in here?" Selena shouted over the music.

"Everyone under forty?" Gen laughed. With a small hand wave Gen put up a minor sound shield, muting the music. "People are going to stir crazy. Combine that with the anniversary—"

The anniversary.

Today.

The day the war had begun, the day the

united fleet had died.

They'd been dying for four hundred years, well aware that the reserve of orun crystals was depleted and there was no way to move forward with the ships they had.

Old Captain Baular had seen the deposit of orun on the fifth planet as their saving grace. He'd get it even if it meant killing the grounders.

And, coward that he was, he'd ordered his grandson to lead the first attack instead of leading it himself.

That opening skirmish began and ended in the dark, with Titan Sciarra in the infirmary, and five Academy fighters mis-sing or damaged. But by lunch of the next day, every officer belonging to crews allied with the Baulars withdrew.

Seven months later, heated words turned to live rounds.

"Selena?" Gen asked quietly, placing a hand on her arm. "You didn't know the date, did you?"

"I was trying not to think about." If she had, she'd have cut her vacation to the islands early. Maybe even made her pilgrimage to the small cay where she'd ditched her stolen fighter after driving off the attack.

She rolled her shoulder, stretching the deep scars. "It snuck up on me."

"First round, we drink to the Lost Fleet, and all who've gone on to crew it. I'm buying," Gen said with a touch of forced joviality. "Carver's been making friends. Tell her, babe." She pushed Carver's shoulder.

Perrin Carver was tall, broad-shouldered man with shy, hazel eyes that hid a wicked sense of humor.

Selena's heart fluttered just a little at the memory of a time when she'd fancied herself in love with him. He'd been the ideal starsider: intelligent, good-looking, and charismatic. They'd been friends of a sort, but even that relationship had soured when she'd realized he'd been getting close to her so he could learn more about Genevieve Silar.

Carver nodded and held out his hand. "Hi, Selena. How are you?"

She tapped the back of his hand with hers, letting him test her shields. "Good. How's the Starguard?"

"Booming." The commander of the Starguard smiled, white teeth flashing, but there was a tightness around his eyes. "Everyone hears about guardians being allowed outside the Enclave, or working with the Jhandarmi, and I'm drowning in recruiting requests. Captains of larger crews invite me to Captain's Mess so they can introduce me to their best and brightest. Half the time I can't tell if they want me to marry into the crew or take the fleetlings into the guard." His shield was still attached to hers, scanning her as he talked.

All he would get from her was polite interest. Her heartrate didn't spike or dip at the mention of the Jhandarmi. Her smile never flickered.

"Maybe you should lock down Gen," Selena said. "If you had a spouse, no one would try to get you to marry into the crew."

Carver and Gen shared a look, and Gen

sent a ping of information that Selena's implant translated as an ongoing debate over crew name and a place to live.

Carver sent something similar; a picture of his bachelor's quarters and his one ship.

There was no room for them to marry and have a family.

"Enclave is a temporary solution," Selena said out loud. She'd lost the taste for communicating by implant years ago. "If we—"

A heavy hand wrapped around her waist as someone wearing too much cologne stepped far too close to her. "Hello, Selena."

Hollis Silar, one of Gen's many siblings, kissed her temple.

Simultaneously, Selena sighed, sent a shock through her shield to Hollis's hand, and elbowed him in the gut. "Hi, Hollis. I see you're still bathing in cologne rather than water."

He stepped away from her, an easy smile still in place.

It wasn't that Hollis was bad looking;

plenty of women found him handsome.

It was that he was equally affectionate with every woman he saw and he couldn't keep a secret to save his life. Or anyone else's.

He'd chase anyone with a pretty smile and fell in and out of love a couple of times a day.

"Nice to see you too, Selena. Now, everyone, you're all going to look at me, smile, and laugh like I'm my normal, dashing self," he said, his smile never changing. "You haven't been paying attention, but I'm not a member of the Starguard for nothing. We're being watched. Now take your nice drinks from the waitress and keep your eyes on me."

Hollis nodded to the waitress and handed out four cups with bright purple liquid. "Bruised Stars all around. Guaranteed to make you giggle, or so the guy at the bar told me. Although he's a Seutaai, so take it with a shield in place." He handed Selena her drink with a smile, but turned immediately to glance over his shoulder.

"Big brother, who are we looking for?" Gen asked with a slow drawl. "Is it a friend who you might have forgotten to call back after a night out?"

Hollis shook his head. "No, I thought I saw some of the Lee crew. Make that, I'm certain of it."

Selena grimaced. "As long as Rowena isn't here."

"Did you call me?"

Startled, Selena looked up to the face of her least favorite woman: Rowena Lee.

"Hello," Selena said politely. "I see you're still alive. That's..."

Unfortunate.

She nodded and took a slug of her Bruised Star.

Rowena held up a tray of electric blue shots. "My crew thinks I can't out-drink anyone in this bar. I probably can't go toe-to-toe with alcoholics like the Silars here. But No-Shot Selena?" Rowena set the drinks on the table. "I can out-shoot you in the stars or on the ground."

Gen sucked in air between her teeth and sent Selena several urgent pings telling her to ignore the Lees.

Selena muted Gen. "I took plenty of shots in the war. As I recall, I disabled three of your big birds. *Bassi, Aryton, Theoano…* Bang, bang, bang." Selena mimed firing with her finger. "Three shots. Three silent ships."

"Not kills," Rowena said. "A whole war and you never blooded yourself."

That was it, the memory she didn't want to face; the time she'd almost taken Death's claim and risked killing someone outside of war.

"That's uncalled for," Hollis said, trying to step between them. "Selena, why don't we—"

Selena pushed Hollis aside and grabbed the first shot.

She tossed back the potent drink and shattered the glass on the table. "Go suck vacuum, Rowena. You're a pissant yeoman with no hope of command."

"I went to the Academy, same as you, Selena. I fought for the fleet." Rowena slammed a shot back. "You fought for the mud-lickers."

Selena took another shot as the first started to fuzz her judgement. "I prevented the Baulars from committing mass genocide and destroying the civilians along with the fleet."

Rowena took her second shot. A crowd was gathering and that seemed to feed her cruelty. "The Lees survived the war. We're still here. How many Caryll captains are there? Oh, right, one. Can you count that high, No-Shot? You have any idea how easy it would be for me to end you right now?"

Selena took the last two glasses and slammed them both back.

Gen pinged her, giving locations, counts, and identities of the Lee allies in the crowd.

Hollis stepped to her flank, ready to defend her.

She stood, anger burning through her veins. "Sure, your crew outnumbers mine. I guess on paper, it's not really a fair fight, is it, Rowena? But you were trained as a flight leader, and what do Carylls do? Hand-to-hand combat. Maybe I should

thin your ranks, starting with one mouthy
yeoman."

Keep reading! Head to:
www.inkprintpress.com/sfrom/malik
/bodies/

ABOUT THE AUTHOR

LIANA BROOKS is a summer child who loves hot days, sultry and humid nights, flowers growing wild, and the sound of summer rain. When she isn't swimming, she enjoys writing science fiction in every form, from sprawling space operas (*Fleet of Malik*) to the antics of a superhero family (*Heroes and Villains*).

You can learn more about her and her books at www.LianaBrooks.com.

INKLETS

Collect them all! Released on the 1st and 15th
of each month.

Welcome to Dark Dale
LIANA BROOKS

When War Came to Town
A Powers Story
AMY LAURENS

Not Fantasy
AMY LAURENS

Courting the Winter Prince
LIANA BROOKS

At the Home of the Winter King
A Storm Foxes Story
AMY LAURENS

With This Ring
AMY LAURENS

Venus &
Seven Reasons I Said No
LIANA BROOKS

OATH KEEPER
AMY LAURENS

FORGET
A Powers Story
AMY LAURENS

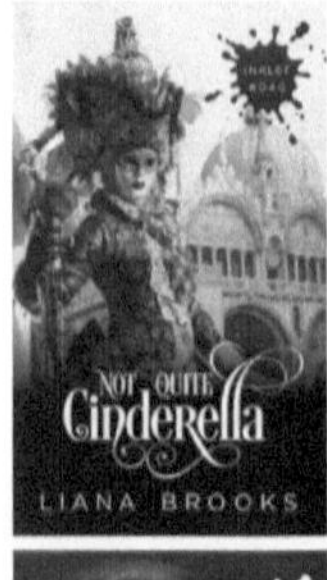
INKLET #040
NOT QUITE
Cinderella
LIANA BROOKS

INKLET #041
ONE BAD MAN
AMY LAURENS

DOUBLE ISSUE
INKLET #042
The Claustrophobia
Of Loneliness &
Adam, Be A Star
AMY LAURENS

INKLET #043
The Artist
as a Young Girl
LIANA BROOKS

INKLET #044
CONFESSIONS
AMY LAURENS

INKLET #045
But For Snow
A Kallista Story
AMY LAURENS

INKLET #046
The Boy
Named NO
LIANA BROOKS

INKLET #047
Anamata
AMY LAURENS

INKLET #048
A Wolf FOR
Christmas
AMY LAURENS